Young Austerlitz

W. G. SEBALD

PENGUIN BOOKS

PENGUIN BOOKS

Published by the Penguin Group
Penguin Books Ltd, 80 Strand, London WC2R 0RL, England
Penguin Group (USA) Inc., 375 Hudson Street, New York, New York 10014, USA
Penguin Group (Canada), 10 Alcorn Avenue, Toronto, Ontario, Canada M4V 3B2
(a division of Pearson Penguin Canada Inc.)
Penguin Ireland, 25 St Stephen's Green, Dublin 2, Ireland
(a division of Penguin Books Ltd)
Penguin Group (Australia), 250 Camberwell Road, Camberwell, Victoria 3124,
Australia (a division of Pearson Australia Group Pty Ltd)
Penguin Books India Pvt Ltd, 11 Community Centre,
Panchsheel Park, New Delhi – 110 017, India
Penguin Group (NZ), cnr Airborne and Rosedale Roads, Albany,
Auckland 1310, New Zealand (a division of Pearson New Zealand Ltd)
Penguin Books (South Africa) (Pty) Ltd, 24 Sturdee Avenue,
Rosebank 2196, South Africa

Penguin Books Ltd, Registered Offices: 80 Strand, London WC2R 0RL, England

www.penguin.com

First published in Germany by Carl Hanser Verlag 2001
First published in Great Britain by Hamish Hamilton 2001
This extract published as a Pocket Penguin 2005

1

Set in 11/13pt Monotype Dante
Typeset by Palimpsest Book Production Limited
Polmont, Stirlingshire
Printed in England by Clays Ltd, St Ives plc

In
1935 if you wanted to
read a good book, you needed
either a lot of money or a library card.
Cheap paperbacks were available, but their
poor production generally mirrored the quality
between the covers. One weekend that year,
Allen Lane, Managing Director of The Bodley Head,
having spent the weekend visiting Agatha Christie,
found himself on a platform at Exeter station trying to
find something to read for his journey back to London.
He was appalled by the quality of the material he had to
choose from. Everything that Allen Lane achieved from that
day until his death in 1970 was based on a passionate belief
in the existence of 'a vast reading public for *intelligent*
books at a low price'. The result of his momentous vision
was the birth not only of Penguin, but of the 'paperback
revolution'. Quality writing became available for the price of
a packet of cigarettes, literature became a mass medium
for the first time, a nation of book-borrowers became a
nation of book-buyers – and the very concept of book
publishing was changed for ever. Those founding
principles – of quality and value, with an overarching
belief in the fundamental importance of reading –
have guided everything the company has
done since 1935. Sir Allen Lane's
pioneering spirit is still very much alive
at Penguin in 2005. Here's to
the next 70 years!

MORE THAN A BUSINESS

'We decided it was time to end the almost customary half-hearted manner in which cheap editions were produced – as though the only people who could possibly want cheap editions must belong to a lower order of intelligence. We, however, believed in the existence in this country of a vast reading public for intelligent books at a low price, and staked everything on it'
Sir Allen Lane, 1902–1970

'The Penguin Books are splendid value for sixpence, so splendid that if other publishers had any sense they would combine against them and suppress them'
George Orwell

'More than a business … a national cultural asset'
Guardian

'When you look at the whole Penguin achievement you know that it constitutes, in action, one of the more democratic successes of our recent social history'
Richard Hoggart

I grew up, began Austerlitz that evening in the bar of the Great Eastern Hotel, in the little country town of Bala in Wales, in the home of a Calvinist preacher and former missionary called Emyr Elias who was married to a timid-natured Englishwoman. I have never liked looking back at the time I spent in that unhappy house, which stood in isolation on a hill just outside the town and was much too large for two people and an only child. Several rooms on the top floor were kept shut up year in, year out. Even today I still sometimes dream that one of those locked doors opens and I step through it, into a friendlier, more familiar world. Several of the rooms that were not locked were unused too. Furnished sparsely with a bed or a chest of drawers, curtains drawn even during the day, they drowsed in a twilight that soon extinguished every sense of self-awareness in me. So I can recall almost nothing of my early days in Bala except how it hurt to be suddenly called by a new name, and how dreadful it was, once my own clothes had disappeared, to have to go around dressed in the English fashion in shorts, knee-length socks which were always slipping down, a string vest like a fish-net and a mouse-grey shirt, much too thin. I know that I often lay awake for hours in my narrow bed in the manse, trying to conjure up the faces of those whom I had left, I feared through my own fault, but not until I was numb with weariness and my eyelids sank in the darkness did I see my mother bending down to me just for a fleeting moment, or my father smiling as he put on his hat. Such comfort made it all the worse to wake up early in the morning and have to face the knowledge, new every day, that I was not at home now but very far away, in some kind of captivity. Only recently have I recalled how oppressed I felt, in all the time I spent with the Eliases, by the fact that they never opened a window, and perhaps that is why when I was out and about some-where on a summer's day years later, and passed a house with all its windows thrown open, I felt an extraordi-nary sense of being carried away and out of myself. It was only a few days ago that, thinking over that expe-rience of liberation, I remembered how one of the two windows of my bedroom was walled up on the inside while it remained unchanged on the outside, a circum-stance which, as one is never both outside and inside a house at the same time, I did not register until I was thirteen or fourteen, although it must have been trou-bling me throughout my childhood in Bala. The manse was always freezing, Austerlitz continued, not just in winter, when the only fire was often in the kitchen stove and the stone floor in the hallway was frequently covered with hoar frost, but in autumn too, and well into spring and the infallibly wet summers. And just as cold reigned in the house in Bala, so did silence. The minister's wife was always busy with her housework, dusting, mopping the tiled floor, doing the laundry, polishing the brass door fittings and preparing the meagre meals which we usually ate without a word. Sometimes she merely walked round the house making sure that everything was in its proper place, from which she would never allow it to be moved. I once found her sitting on a chair in one of the half-empty rooms upstairs, with tears in her eyes and a crumpled wet handkerchief in her hand. When she saw me standing in the doorway she rose and said it was nothing, she had only caught a cold, and as she went out she ran her fingers through my hair, the one time, as far as I remember, she ever did such a thing. Meanwhile it was the minister's unalterable custom to sit in his study, which had a view of a dark corner of the garden, thinking about next Sunday's sermon. He never wrote any of these sermons down, but worked them out in his head, toiling over them for at least four days. He would always emerge from his study in the evening in a state of deep despondency, only to disappear into it again next morning. But on Sunday, when he stood up in chapel in front of his congregation and often addressed them for a full hour, he was a changed man; he spoke with a moving eloquence which I still feel I can hear, conjuring up before the eyes of his flock the Last Judgment awaiting them all, the lurid fires of purgatory, the torments of damnation and then, with the most wonderful stellar and celestial imagery, the entry of the righteous into eternal bliss. With apparent ease, as if he were making up the most appalling horrors as he went along, he always succeeded in filling the hearts of his congregation with such sentiments of remorse that at the end of the service quite a number of them went home looking white as a sheet. The minister himself, on the other hand, was in a comparatively jovial mood for the rest of Sunday. At midday dinner, which always began with tapioca soup, he would make a few informative and semi-jocular remarks to his wife, who was exhausted from cooking the meal, inquired after my welfare, generally by asking, 'And how is the boy?', and tried to draw me out a little. The meal always finished with the minister's favourite dish of rice pudding, and he usually fell silent as he enjoyed it. Once dinner was over he lay down on the sofa to rest for an hour, or in fine weather he would sit out under the apple tree in the front garden looking down the valley, as well satisfied with his week's work as the Lord God of Sabaoth after the creation of the world. Before evening prayers he went to his roll-top desk and took out the tin box in which he kept the calendar published by the Calvinist Methodists of Wales, a grey little book already worn rather threadbare and listing the Sundays and church festivals for the years 1928 to 1946, in which he had made regular entries against every date week by week, removing the thin solid-ink pencil from the back of the book, moistening its tip with his tongue, and very slowly and neatly, like a schoolboy under supervision, noting down the name of the chapel where he had preached that day and the biblical passage he had taken as his text, for instance, under 20 July 1939: The Tabernacle, Llandrillo – *Psalms* CLXVII, 4, 'He telleth the number of the stars: he calleth them all by their names'; under 3 August 1941: Chapel Uchaf, Gilboa – *Zephaniah* III, 6, 'I have cut off the nations: their towers are desolate; I made their streets waste, that none passeth by'; and under 21 May 1944: Chapel Bethesda, Corwen – *Isaiah* XLVIII, 18, 'O that thou hadst hearkened to my commandments! then had thy peace been as a river and thy righteousness as the waves of the sea!' The last entry in this little book, which is among those few of the minister's possessions to have passed into my hands after his death and through which I have often glanced recently, said Austerlitz, was made on one of the additional leaves inserted at the end and is dated 7 March 1952. It runs: Bala Chapel – *Psalms* CII, 6, 'I am like a pelican of the wilderness: I am like an owl of the desert.' For the most part, of course, these Sunday sermons, and I must have heard over five hundred of them, went over my head when I was a child, but even if the meaning of the various words and phrases was a mystery to me for a long time, and whether Elias delivered them in English or Welsh, I did understand that his subject was the sinfulness and punishment of mankind, fire and ashes and the approaching end of the world. However, said Austerlitz, in my memory Calvinist eschatology is linked not so much to these biblical images of destruction as to what I saw with my own eyes when I was out with Elias. Many of his younger colleagues in the ministry had been called up into the army soon after the beginning of the war, and consequently at least every other Sunday he had to go and preach to another congregation, often quite a long way off. At first we drove across country in a little two-seater trap drawn by an almost snow-white pony, and in accordance with Elias's usual custom he would sit hunched up in the blackest of moods on the outward journey. On the way back, however, his spirits rose, just as they did at home on Sunday afternoons; he sometimes even hummed to himself, and cracked the whip around the pony's ears now and then. And these light and dark sides of the minister Elias were reflected in the mountainous landscape around us. I remember, said Austerlitz, how we were once driving through the endless Tanat valley, with nothing on the hillsides to right and left of us but crooked bushes, ferns and rusty-hued vegetation, and then, for the last part of the way up to the col, only grey rock and drifting mist, so that I was afraid we were coming to the very ends of the earth. But on another day, when we had just reached the Pennant pass I saw a gap open up in the banked clouds towering high in the west, and the rays of the sun cast a narrow beam of light down to the valley floor lying at a dizzying depth below us. Where there had been nothing a moment ago but fathomless gloom, there now shone a little village with a few orchards, meadows and fields, surrounded by black shadows but sparkling green like the Islands of the Blest, and as we walked down the road from the pass beside the pony and trap everything grew lighter and lighter, the mountain sides emerged from the darkness shining brightly, the fine grasses bending in the wind shimmered with light, the silvery willows gleamed down on the banks of the stream; before long we had descended from the barren heights and found ourselves among trees and bushes again, beneath the softly rustling oaks and maples, and rowans already laden with red berries. Once, I think when I was nine, I went away with Elias to a place in South Wales where the flanks of the mountains had been ripped open on both sides of the road, and the woods mauled and cut down. I don't remember the name of the village we reached at nightfall. It was surrounded by pithead stocks of coal spilling down into the alleys here and there. We had been given a room in the house of one of the church elders, from which there was a view of a winding-tower with a gigantic wheel turning now this way and now that in the gathering dusk, and further down the valley tall flames and showers of sparks shot high into the sky from the smelting furnaces of an iron and steel works, at regular intervals of about three or four minutes. When I was in bed Elias sat on a stool by the window, looking out in silence for a long time. I think that it was the sight of the valley first illuminated by the firelight, then sinking back into darkness, which inspired him to preach on a text from Revelation next morning, delivering a sermon on the wrath of the Lord, on the war and the devastation of the dwellings of men, a diatribe in which, so the elder told him when we left, he had surpassed himself. If the congregation had been almost petrified by terror during the sermon, I myself could hardly have had the divine power invoked by Elias more permanently impressed on my mind than by the fact that a bomb had dropped in broad daylight that afternoon in the little town at the end of the valley, where Elias was to take evening prayers that same day. The ruins were still smouldering when we reached the centre of the town, and people were standing about in the road in small groups, some with their hands still raised to their mouths in horror. The fire engine had driven straight across a round flower-bed, and there on the grass, dressed in their Sunday best, lay the bodies of those who, as I hardly needed Elias to tell me, had sinned against the Lord's commandment to keep the Sabbath day holy. In this way a kind of Old Testament mythology of retribution gradually built up inside my head, and I always saw its supreme expression in the submersion of the village of Llanwddyn beneath the waters of the Vyrnwy reservoir. As far as I can remember it was on the way back from one of his journeys to preach away from home, at either Abertridwr or Pont Llogel, that Elias stopped the pony-trap on the banks of this lake and walked out with me to the middle of the dam, where he told me about his family home lying down there at a depth of about a hundred feet under the dark water, and not just his own family home but at least forty other houses and farms, together with the church of St John of Jerusalem, three chapels and three pubs, all of them drowned when the dam was finished in the autumn of 1888. In the years before its submersion, so Elias had told him, said Austerlitz, Llanwddyn had been particularly famous for its games of football on the village green when the full moon shone in summer, often lasting all night and played by over ten dozen youths and men of almost every age, some of them from neighbouring villages. The story of the football games of Llanwddyn occupied my imagination for a long time, said Austerlitz, first and foremost, I am sure, because Elias never told me anything else about his own life either before or afterwards. At this one moment on the Vyrnwy dam when, intentionally or unintentionally, he allowed me a glimpse into his clerical heart, I felt for him so much that he, the righteous man, seemed to me like the only survivor of the deluge which had destroyed Llanwddyn, while I imagined all the others – his parents, his brothers and sisters, his relations, their neighbours, all the other villagers – still down in the depths, sitting in their houses and walking along the road, but unable to speak and with their eyes opened far too wide. This notion of mine about the sub-aquatic existence of the people of Llanwddyn also had something to do with the album which Elias first showed me on our return home that evening, containing several photographs of his birthplace, now sunk beneath the water. As there were no other pictures of any kind in the manse, I leafed

again and again through these few photographs, which came into my own possession only much later along with the Calvinist calendar, until the people looking out of them, the blacksmith in his leather apron, Elias's father the sub-postmaster, the shepherd walking along the village street with his sheep, and most of all the girl sitting in a chair in the garden with her little dog on her lap, became as familiar to me as if I were living with them down at the bottom of the lake. At night, before

I fell asleep in my cold room, I often felt as if I too had been submerged in that dark water, and like the poor souls of Vyrnwy must keep my eyes wide open to catch a faint glimmer of light far above me, and see the

reflection, broken by ripples, of the stone tower standing in such fearsome isolation on the wooded bank.
Sometimes I even imagined that I had seen one or other
of the people from the photographs in the album walking down the road in Bala, or out in the fields, particularly around noon on hot summer days, when there was
no one else about and the air flickered hazily. Elias said
I was not to speak of such things, so instead I spent
every free moment I could with Evan the cobbler, whose
workshop was not far from the manse and who had a
reputation for seeing ghosts. I also learned Welsh from
Evan, picking it up very quickly, because I liked his
stories much better than the endless psalms and biblical verses I had to learn by heart for Sunday school.
Unlike Elias, who always connected illness and death
with tribulations, just punishment and guilt, Evan told
tales of the dead who had been struck down by fate
untimely, who knew they had been cheated of what was
due to them and tried to return to life. If you had an
eye for them they were to be seen quite often, said Evan.
At first glance they seemed to be normal people, but
when you looked more closely their faces would blur
or flicker slightly at the edges. And they were usually a
little shorter than they had been in life, for the experi-
ence of death, said Evan, diminishes us, just as a piece
of linen shrinks when you first wash it. The dead almost
always walked alone, but they did sometimes go around
in small troops; they had been seen wearing brightly
coloured uniforms or wrapped in grey cloaks, march-
ing up the hill above the town to the soft beat of a drum,
and only a little taller than the walls round the fields

through which they went. Evan told me the story of how his grandfather once had to step aside on the road from Frongastell to Pyrsau to let one of these ghostly processions pass by when it caught up with him. It had consisted entirely of beings of dwarfish stature who strode on at a fast pace, leaning forward slightly and talking to each other in reedy voices. Hanging from a hook on the wall above Evan's low workbench, said Austerlitz, was the black veil that his grandfather had taken from the bier when the small figures muffled in their cloaks carried it past him, and it was certainly Evan, said Austerlitz, who once told me that nothing but a piece of silk like that separates us from the next world. It is a fact that through all the years I spent at the manse in Bala I never shook off the feeling that something very obvious, very manifest in itself was hidden from me. Sometimes it was as if I were in a dream and trying to perceive reality; then again I felt as if an invisible twin brother were walking beside me, the reverse of a shadow, so to speak. And I suspected that some meaning relating to myself lay behind the Bible stories I was given to read in Sunday school from my sixth year onwards, a meaning quite different from the sense of the printed words as I ran my index finger along the lines. I can still see myself, said Austerlitz, muttering intently and spelling out the story of Moses again and again from the large-print children's edition of the Bible Miss Parry had given me when I had been set to learn by heart the chapter about the confounding of the languages of the earth, and succeeded in reciting it correctly and with good expression. I have only to turn a couple of pages of that book, said Austerlitz, to remember how anxious I felt at the time when I read the tale of the daughter of Levi, who made an ark of bulrushes and daubed it with slime and with pitch, placed the child in the ark and laid it among the reeds by the side of the water – *yn yr hesg ar fin yr afon*, I think that was how it ran. Further on in the story of Moses, said Austerlitz, I particularly liked the episode where the children of Israel cross a terrible wilderness, many days' journey long and wide, with nothing in sight but sky and sand as far as the eye can see. I tried to picture the pillar of cloud going before the people on their wanderings 'to lead them the way', as the Bible puts it, and I immersed myself, forgetting all around me, in a full-page illustration showing the desert of Sinai looking just like the part of Wales where I grew up, with bare mountains crowding close together and a grey-hatched background, which I took sometimes for the sea and sometimes for the air above it. And indeed, said Austerlitz on a later occasion when he showed me his Welsh children's Bible, I knew that my proper place was among the tiny figures populating the camp. I examined every square inch of the illustration, which seemed to me uncannily familiar. I thought I could make out a stone quarry in a rather lighter patch on the steep slope of the mountain over to the right, and I seemed to see a railway track in the regular curve of the lines below it. But my mind dwelt chiefly on the fenced square in the middle and the tent-like building at the far end, with a cloud of white smoke above it. Whatever may have been going on inside me at the time, the children of

Israel's camp in the wilderness was closer to me than life in Bala, which I found more incomprehensible every day, or at least, said Austerlitz, that is how it strikes me now. That evening in the bar of the Great Eastern Hotel Austerlitz also told me that there was no wireless set or newspaper in the manse in Bala. I don't know that Elias and his wife Gwendolyn ever mentioned the fighting on the continent of Europe, he said: I couldn't imagine any world outside Wales. Only after the end of the war did this state of affairs begin to change. A new epoch seemed to dawn with the victory celebrations, when even in Bala there was dancing in the streets, which were decked with brightly coloured bunting. For me, it began when I first broke the ban on going to the cinema, and after that I used to watch the newsreel from the cubbyhole occupied by the film projectionist Owen, one of the three sons of the visionary Evan. Around the same time Gwendolyn's state of health deteriorated, almost imperceptibly at first but then with increasing speed. She, who had always kept everything in the most painfully neat order, began to neglect first the house and then herself. She simply stood in the kitchen, looking helpless, and when Elias prepared a meal as best he could she would eat almost nothing. Her illness was certainly the reason why I was sent to a private school near Oswestry in the autumn term of 1946, when I was twelve years old. Like most such educational establishments, Stower Grange was the most unsuitable place imaginable for an adolescent. The headmaster, a man called Penrith-Smith, who wandered aimlessly about the school buildings in his dusty gown all day from early morning until late at night, was hopelessly forgetful and absent-minded, and the rest of the teaching staff in that immediate post-war period were also a curious collection of oddities, most of them over sixty or suffering from some affliction. School life ran more or less of its own accord, not so much thanks to the masters who taught us at Stower Grange as in spite of them, and certainly not by virtue of any particular ethos but through customs and traditions, a number of them positively oriental in character, going back over many generations of pupils. There were all kinds of forms of major tyranny and minor despotism, forced labour, enslavement, serfdom, the bestowal and withdrawal of privileges, hero-worship, ostracism, the imposition of penalties and the granting of reprieves, and by dint of these the pupils, without any supervision, governed themselves and indeed the entire school, not excluding the masters. Even when Penrith-Smith, a remarkably kindly man, did have to chastise one of us in his office for some reason which had been brought to his notice, you could easily have gained the impression that the victim was temporarily granting the headmaster who inflicted the punishment a privilege due in fact only to him, the boy who had reported to take it. Sometimes, particularly at weekends, it seemed as if all the masters had gone away leaving the pupils in their care to their own devices in the school, which was at least two miles outside town. Then some of us would wander about at our own sweet will, while others hatched plots to extend their power bases, or went to the laboratory furnished only with a few rickety benches and stools at the end of the dark basement corridor known, for some inexplicable reason, as the Red Sea, to toast bread and make scrambled eggs from a sulphur-yellow powdered egg substitute, a large supply of which was kept in one of the wall cupboards, along with other substances intended for chemistry lessons. Given the conditions at Stower Grange, of course, quite a number of boys spent all their schooldays there in a state of misery. For instance, said Austerlitz, I remember a boy called Robinson, who was obviously so unable to reconcile himself to the harshness and idiosyncrasies of school life that at the age of nine or ten he tried, on several occasions, to run away in the middle of the night by climbing down a drainpipe and striking out across country. A policeman always brought him back next morning in the check dressing-gown which, curiously, he must have put on especially for his flight, and handed him over to the headmaster like a common criminal. However, unlike poor Robinson, said Austerlitz, I myself found my years at Stower Grange a time not of imprisonment but of liberation. While most of us, even those who tormented their contemporaries, crossed off the days on the calendar until they could go home, I would have preferred never to return to Bala at all. From the very first week I realized that for all the adversities of the school it was my only escape route, and I immediately did all I could to find my way around its strange jumble of countless unwritten rules, and the often almost carnivalesque lawlessness that prevailed. It was a great advantage that I soon began to distinguish myself on the rugby field, perhaps because a dull pain always present within me, although I was unaware of it at the time, enabled me to lower my head and make my way through ranks of opponents better than any of my fellow pupils. The fearlessness I displayed in rugger matches, as I remember them always played under a cold winter sky or in pouring rain, very soon gave me special status without my having to try for it by other means, such as recruiting vassals or enslaving weaker boys. Another crucial factor in my good progress at school was the fact that I never found reading and studying a burden. Far from it, for confined as I had been until now to the Bible in Welsh and homiletic literature, it seemed as if a new door were opening whenever I turned a page. I read everything in the school library, which contained an entirely arbitrary selection of works, and everything I could borrow from my teachers – works on geography and history, travel writings, novels, biographies – and sat up until late in the evening over reference books and atlases. My mind thus gradually created a kind of ideal landscape in which the Arabian desert, the realm of the Aztecs, the continent of Antarctica, the snow-covered Alps, the North-West Passage, the river Congo and the Crimean peninsula formed a single panorama, populated by all the figures proper to those places. As I could move into that world at any time I liked – in a Latin lesson, during divine service, on the interminable weekends – I never fell into the depression from which so many of the boys at Stower Grange suffered. I felt miserable only when it was time to go home for the holidays. Even on my first return to Bala at half-term on All Saints' Day, I felt as if my life were once again under the unlucky star which had been my companion as long as I could remember. Gwendolyn had gone further downhill during my two months' absence. She now lay in bed all day looking fixedly up at the ceiling. Elias came in to see her for a while every morning and every evening, but neither he nor Gwendolyn spoke a single word. It seems to me now, looking back, said Austerlitz, as if they were slowly being killed by the chill in their hearts. I don't know what kind of illness Gwendolyn died of, and I suspect that she herself could not have said. At least, she had no weapon against it but the curious compulsion which came over her several times a day, and perhaps during the night too, to powder herself with a kind of cheap talc from a large container standing on the little table beside her bed. Gwendolyn used such quantities of this powder, fine as dust and slightly greasy, that the linoleum floor around her bed, and soon the whole room and the corridors of the upper storey as well, were covered with a white layer, slightly sticky because of the damp air. I only recently remembered this white pall over the manse, said Austerlitz, when I was reading the reminiscences of his childhood and youth by a Russian writer who describes a similar mania for powder in his grandmother, a lady who, although she spent most of her time lying on a sofa nourishing herself almost exclusively on wine gums and almond milk, enjoyed an iron constitution and always slept with her window wide open, so that once, after a night of stormy weather, she woke up in the morning under a blanket of snow without coming to the slightest harm. However, it was different in the manse. The sick-room windows were kept closed, and the white powder which had settled on everything, grain by grain, and through which visible paths had now been trodden, was not at all like glittering snow. Rather, it resembled the ectoplasm that, as Evan had once told me, clairvoyants can produce from their mouths in great bubbles which then fall to the ground, where they soon dry and fall to dust. No, it was not newly fallen snow wafting around the manse; what filled it was something unpleasant, and I did not know where it came from, only much later and in another book finding for it the completely incomprehensible but to me, said Austerlitz, immediately enlightening term 'arsanical horror'. It was during the coldest winter in human memory that I came home for the second time from the school in Oswestry, and found Gwendolyn barely alive. There was a coal fire smouldering on the hearth of her sick-room. The yellowish smoke that rose from the glowing coals and never entirely dispersed up the chimney mingled with the smell of carbolic pervading the whole house. I stood for hours at the window, studying the wonderful formations of icy mountain ranges two or three inches high formed above the crossbars by water running down the panes. Now and then solitary figures emerged from the snowy landscape outside. Wrapped in dark scarves and shawls, umbrellas open to keep off the flurry of snowflakes, they stumbled up the hill. I heard them knocking the snow off their boots down in the porch before they slowly climbed the stairs, escorted by the neighbour's daughter who was now keeping house for the minister. With a certain hesitancy, and as if they had to bend underneath something, they stepped over the threshold and put whatever they had brought – a jar of pickled red cabbage, a can of corned beef, a bottle of rhubarb wine – down on the chest of drawers. Gwendolyn took no notice of these visitors, and the visitors themselves dared not look at her. They usually stood at the window with me for a little while, looking out too, and sometimes cleared their throats slightly. When they had gone again, it was as quiet as before except for the shallow breathing I could hear behind me, and an eternity seemed to pass between each breath. On Christmas Day, making a great effort, Gwendolyn sat up in bed once more. Elias had brought her a cup of sweet tea, but she only moistened her lips with it. Then she said, so quietly that you could hardly hear her: What was it that so darkened our world? And Elias replied: I don't know, dear, I don't know. Gwendolyn lingered until the New Year. On Epiphany Day, however, she reached the final stage. The cold had grown stronger than ever outside, and it had become more and more silent. The whole country, so I heard later, came to a standstill that winter. Even Lake Bala, which I had thought as big as the ocean when I arrived in Wales, was covered by a thick sheet of ice. I thought of the roach and eels in its depths, and the birds which the visitors had told me were falling from the branches of the trees, frozen stiff. It was never really light in these days, and when at last, very far away, the sun shone faintly in the misty blue sky, the dying woman opened her eyes wide and would not move her glance from the weak light filtering through the window panes. Only when darkness fell did she lower her lids, and not long after that a gurgling sound began to emerge from her throat with every breath she took. I sat beside her all night, together with the minister. At dawn the stertorous breathing stopped. Gwendolyn's body arched slightly and then sank back again. It was a kind of tensing movement; I had felt it once before, when I picked up an injured rabbit from the headland of a field, and its heart stopped in my hand for fear. But directly after she had arched herself in death Gwendolyn's body seemed to shrink a little, reminding me of what Evan had told me. I saw her eyes sink back in their sockets, and her thin lips, now stretched tautly back, half-bared her crooked bottom teeth, while outside, for the first time in many days, the rose-coloured light of dawn touched the rooftops of Bala. I don't remember exactly how the rest of that day passed after she died, said Austerlitz. I think I was so exhausted that I lay down and slept very deeply for a very long time. When I got up again, Gwendolyn was already in her coffin, which stood on the four mahogany chairs in the front room. She was wearing her wedding dress, kept all these years in a trunk upstairs, and a pair of white gloves with a great many little mother of pearl buttons which I had never seen before. The sight of them brought tears into my eyes, the first tears I had ever shed in the manse. Elias was sitting beside the coffin keeping watch over the dead woman, while on his own out in the empty barn, which creaked with the frost, the young assistant minister who had ridden over from Corwen on a pony was rehearsing the sermon he would preach on the day of the funeral. Elias never recovered from his wife's death.

Grief is not the right word for the condition into which he had fallen since she lay dying, said Austerlitz. Although I did not understand it at the time, as a boy of thirteen, I can see now that the unhappiness building up inside him had destroyed his faith just when he needed it most. When I came home again in the summer, it was weeks since he had been able to carry out his duties as a minister. He climbed into the pulpit once more, opened the Bible, and in a broken voice, as if reading to himself alone, announced his text from Lamentations: 'He has made me dwell in darkness as those who have been long dead.' Elias did not preach the sermon itself. He merely stood there for a while, looking out over the heads of his congregation, who were paralysed by alarm, with what seemed to me the motionless eyes of one blinded. Then he slowly climbed down from the pulpit and left the chapel. He was taken away to Denbigh before the end of that summer. I visited him there only once, just before Christmas, with one of the elders of the congregation. The patients were accommodated in a large stone building, and I remember, said Austerlitz, that we had to wait in a room painted green. After quarter of an hour or so, an attendant came and took us up to Elias, who was lying in a bed with railings, his face to the wall. The attendant said: Your son's here to see you, *parech*, but even when he was addressed a second and a third time Elias did not answer. When we left the ward again one of the other inmates, a grey little man with tangled hair, plucked my sleeve and whispered behind his hand: He's not the full shilling, you know – which at the time, curiously enough, said Austerlitz, I felt was a reassuring diagnosis and made the whole wretched situation tolerable. – More than a year after my visit to the Denbigh asylum, at the beginning of the summer term of 1949, when we were just preparing for the exams which would determine our subsequent careers, said Austerlitz, resuming his narrative after a certain time, the headmaster Penrith-Smith summoned me to his study one morning. I can still see him in his frayed gown, wreathed in the blue tobacco smoke from his pipe, standing in the sunlight that slanted in through the small panes of the lead-glazed window and repeating several times in various ways, in his typically confused manner, that in the circumstances my conduct had been exemplary, truly exemplary, given the events of the last two years, and if in the next few weeks I came up to my teachers' expectations of me, which were undoubtedly justified, the Stower Grange trustees would award me a sixth-form scholarship. First, however, it was his duty to tell me that I must put not Dafydd Elias but Jacques Austerlitz on my exam papers. It appears, said Penrith-Smith, that this is your real name. My foster parents, with whom he had discussed the matter at length when I entered the school, had meant to tell me about my origins in good time before the examinations, and if possible adopt me, but as matters now stood, said Penrith-Smith, that was unfortunately out of the question. All he knew himself was that the Eliases had taken me into their house at the beginning of the war, when I was only a little boy, so he could tell me no more. He was sure it would all be settled once Elias's condition improved. As far as the other boys are concerned, said Penrith-Smith, you remain Dafydd Elias for the time being. There's no need to let anyone know. It's just that you will have to put Jacques Austerlitz on your examination papers or else your work may be considered invalid. Penrith-Smith had written the name on a piece of paper, and when he handed it to me I could think of nothing to say, said Austerlitz, but 'Thank you, sir.' At first, what disconcerted me most was that I could connect no ideas at all with the word Austerlitz. If my new name had been Morgan or Jones, I could have related it to reality. I even knew the name Jacques from a French nursery rhyme. But I had never heard of an Austerlitz before, and from the first I was convinced that no one else bore that name, no one in Wales, or in the Isles, or anywhere else in the world. And since I began investigating my own history some years ago, I have never in fact come upon another Austerlitz, not in the telephone books of London or Paris, Amsterdam or Antwerp. But not long ago, turning on the wireless, I happened upon an announcer saying that Fred Astaire, of whom I had previously known nothing at all, was born with the surname of Austerlitz. Astaire's father, who according to this surprising radio programme came from Vienna, had worked as a master brewer in Omaha, Nebraska, where Astaire was born, and from the veranda of the Austerlitz family's house you could hear freight trains being shunted back and forth in the city's marshalling yard. Astaire is reported to have said later that this constant, uninterrupted shunting sound, and the ideas it suggested of going on a long railroad journey, were his only early childhood memories. And just a couple of days after I chanced in this way upon the story of a man entirely unknown to me, Austerlitz added, a neighbour who describes herself as a passionate reader told me that in Kafka's diaries she had found a small, bow-legged man of my own name who, as Kafka recorded, had been called in to circumcise his nephew. I feel it is unlikely that these trails lead anywhere, nor do I entertain any hopes of a note I found some time ago in a file on the practice of euthanasia, mentioning one Laura Austerlitz who made a statement to an Italian investigating judge on 28 June 1966 about the crimes committed in a rice mill on the peninsula of San Saba near Trieste in 1944. At least, said Austerlitz, I haven't yet succeeded in tracking down this namesake of mine. I don't even know if she is still alive, thirty years after making her statement. But personally, as I was saying, I had never heard the name Austerlitz before that April day in 1949 when Penrith-Smith handed me the piece of paper on which he had written it. I couldn't work out the spelling, and read the strange term which sounded to me like some password three or four times, syllable by syllable, before I looked up and said: Excuse me, sir, but what does it mean? To which Penrith-Smith replied: I think you will find it is a small place in Moravia, site of a famous battle, you know. And sure enough, the Moravian village of Austerlitz was discussed at great length during the next school year, for the curriculum in the Lower Sixth included European history, generally regarded as a complicated and not entirely safe subject, so that as a rule it was confined to the period from 1789 to 1814 which ended with a great English victory. The master who was to teach us this period – both glorious and terrible, as he often emphasized – was one André Hilary, who had only just taken up his post at Stower Grange after being demobbed and who, as it soon turned out, was familiar with every detail of the Napoleonic era. André Hilary had studied at Oriel College, but had grown up surrounded by an enthusiasm for Napoleon going back through several generations of his family. His father, so he once told me, said Austerlitz, had him baptized André in memory of Marshal Masséna, duke of Rivoli. Hilary could trace the orbit of the Corsican comet, as he put it, across the sky from its very beginning to its extinction in the South Atlantic Ocean, enumerating all the constellations through which it passed, and the events and characters on which it cast light at any point of its ascendancy or decline, speaking without any preparation and just as if he had been there himself. The Emperor's childhood in Ajaccio, his studies at the military academy of Brienne, the siege of Toulon, the stresses and strains of the Egyptian expedition and his return over a sea full of enemy ships, the crossing of the Great St Bernard, the battles of Marengo, Jena and Auerstedt, of Eylau and Friedland, of Wagram, Leipzig and Waterloo – Hilary brought it all vividly to life for us, partly by recounting the course of these events, often passing from plain narrative to dramatic descriptions and then on to a kind of impromptu performance distributed among several different roles, from one to another of which he switched back and forth with astonishing virtuosity, and partly by studying the gambits of Napoleon and his opponents with the cold intelligence of a non-partisan strategist, surveying the entire landscape of those years from above with an eagle eye, as he once and not without pride remarked. Most of us were deeply impressed by Hilary's history lessons, not least, said Austerlitz, because very often, probably owing to his suffering from slipped discs, he gave them while lying on his back on the floor, nor did we find this at all comic, for it was at such times that Hilary spoke with particular clarity and authority. His undoubted *pièce de résistance* was the battle of Austerlitz. He spoke on it at length, describing the terrain, the highway leading east from Brünn to Olmütz, with the hilly Moravian countryside on its left and the Pratzen heights on its right, the curious cone-shaped mountain which reminded the veterans in the Napoleonic army of the Egyptian pyramids, the villages of Bellwitz, Skolnitz and Kobelnitz, the game park and pheasant enclosure, the watercourse of the Goldbach and the pools and lakes to the south, the French encampment as well as that of the ninety thousand Allies, which extended over a length of nine miles. Hilary told us, said Austerlitz, how at seven in the morning the peaks of the highest hills emerged from the mist like islands in a sea and, as the day gradually grew brighter over the rounded hilltops, the milky haze in the valleys became noticeably denser. The Russian and Austrian troops had come down from the mountain sides like a slow avalanche, and soon, increasingly unsure where they were going, were wandering around on the slopes and in the meadows below, while the French, in a single onslaught, captured

the now half-abandoned positions on the Pratzen
heights and then proceeded to attack the enemy in the
rear from that vantage point. Hilary painted us a
picture of the disposition of the regiments in their
white and red, green and blue uniforms, constantly
forming into new patterns in the course of the battle
like crystals of glass in a kaleidoscope. Again and again
we heard the names of Kolovrat and Bragation,
Kutusov, Bernadotte, Miloradovich, Soult, Murat, Van-
damme and Kellermann, we saw the black clouds of
smoke hovering over the guns, the cannonballs flying
past above the heads of the troops, the glint of bayo-
nets as the first rays of the sun penetrated the mist; we
even seemed to hear the heavy cavalry clashing, and felt
(like a weakness sensed in our own bodies) whole ranks
of men collapsing beneath the surge of the oncoming
force. Hilary could talk for hours about the second of
December 1805, but none the less it was his opinion that
he had to cut his accounts far too short, because, as he
several times told us, it would take an endless length of
time to describe the events of such a day properly, in
some inconceivably complex form recording who had
perished, who survived, and exactly where and how, or
simply saying what the battlefield was like at nightfall,
with the screams and groans of the wounded and dying.
In the end all anyone could ever do was sum up the
unknown factors in the ridiculous phrase, 'The fortunes
of battle swayed this way and that', or some similarly
feeble and useless cliché. All of us, even when we think
we have noted every tiny detail, resort to set pieces
which have already been staged often enough by others.

We try to reproduce the reality, but the harder we try, the more we find the pictures that make up the stock-in-trade of the spectacle of history forcing themselves upon us: the fallen drummer boy, the infantryman shown in the act of stabbing another, the horse's eye starting from its socket, the invulnerable Emperor surrounded by his generals, a moment frozen still amidst the turmoil of battle. Our concern with history, so Hilary's thesis ran, is a concern with pre-formed images already imprinted on our brains, images at which we keep staring while the truth lies elsewhere, away from it all, somewhere as yet undiscovered. I myself, added Austerlitz, in spite of all the accounts of it I have read, remember only the picture of the final defeat of the Allies in the battle of the Three Emperors. Every attempt to understand the course of events inevitably turns into that one scene where the hosts of Russian and Austrian soldiers are fleeing on foot and horseback on to the frozen Satschen ponds. I see cannonballs suspended for an eternity in the air, I see others crashing into the ice, I see the unfortunate victims flinging up their arms as they slide from the toppling floes, and I see them, strangely, not with my own eyes but with those of short-sighted Marshal Davout, who has made a forced march with his regiments from Vienna and, glasses tied firmly behind his head with two laces, looks like an early motorist or aviator. When I look back at André Hilary's performances today, said Austerlitz, I remember once again the idea I developed at the time of being linked in some mysterious way to the glorious past of the people of France. The more often Hilary mentioned the word Austerlitz in front of the class, the more it really did become my own name, and the more clearly I thought I saw that what had at first seemed like an ignominious flaw was changing into a bright light always hovering before me, as promising as the sun of Austerlitz itself when it rose above the December mists. All that school year I felt as if I had been chosen, and although, as I also knew, such a belief in no way matched my uncertain status, I have held fast to it almost my whole life. I don't think that any of my fellow pupils at Stower Grange knew my new name, and the masters, who had been informed of my double identity by Penrith-Smith, went on calling me Elias too. André Hilary was the only one to whom I myself told my real name. It was soon after we had handed in an essay on the concepts of empire and nation that Hilary summoned me to his study outside regular school hours to return my work, which he had marked with a triple-starred A, giving it back in person and not, as he put it, along with everyone else's pathetic efforts. He himself had published various articles in historical journals, and he said he could not have written such a perceptive piece in so comparatively short a space of time; he wondered whether I had perhaps been initiated into historical studies at home by my father or an elder brother. When I answered Hilary's question I had some difficulty in not losing my command over myself, and it was in this situation, which I felt I could no longer endure, that I told him the secret of my real name. It was some time before he was able to calm down. He struck his forehead again and again, breaking into exclamations of astonishment, as if Providence had finally sent him the pupil he had always wanted. For the rest of my time at Stower Grange, Hilary supported and encouraged me in every possible way. I owe it to him first and foremost, said Austerlitz, that I far outstripped the rest of my year in our final examinations in history, Latin, German and French, and could go on my own way into freedom, as I confidently thought at the time, provided with a generous scholarship. When we said goodbye André Hilary gave me a present from his collection of Napoleonic memorabilia, a gold-framed piece of dark card on which, behind shining glass, were fixed three rather fragile willow leaves from a tree on the island of St Helena, along with a scrap of lichen resembling a pale sprig of coral taken by one of Hilary's forebears, as the tiny caption said, from the heavy granite tombstone of Marshal Ney on 31 July 1830. This memento, worth nothing in itself, is still in my possession, said Austerlitz. It means more to me than almost any other picture, first because despite their fragility the relics preserved in it, the lichen and the dried lanceolate willow leaves, have remained intact for more than a century, but also because it reminds me daily of Hilary, without whom I would surely never have been able to emerge from the shadows of the manse in Bala. Moreover, it was Hilary who, after my foster-father's death in the Denbigh asylum early in 1954, undertook the task of winding up his meagre estate and then set on foot the process of my naturalization, which in view of the fact that Elias had obliterated every indication of my origin involved a good deal of difficulty. When I was studying at Oriel, like Hilary himself before me, he visited me regularly, and we took every opportunity of making excursions to the deserted and dilapidated country houses to be found all around Oxford, as elsewhere, in the post-war years. While I was still at school, said Austerlitz, as well as Hilary's support my friendship with Gerald Fitzpatrick in particular helped me to overcome the self-doubts that sometimes oppressed me. In line with the usual practice at public schools, Gerald was assigned to me as a fag when I entered the sixth form. It was his job to keep my room tidy, clean my boots, and bring the tray with the tea things. From the first day, when he asked me for one of the new photographs of the rugger team where I featured to the extreme right of the front row, I realized that Gerald felt as isolated as I did, said Austerlitz, who scarcely a week after our reunion at the Great Eastern Hotel sent me a postcard copy of the picture he had mentioned, without further comment. On that December evening, however, in the

hotel bar, which was quiet now, Austerlitz went on to tell me more about Gerald, and how he had suffered from awful homesickness ever since his arrival at Stower Grange, entirely against the grain of his naturally cheerful disposition. All the time, said Austerlitz, in every free moment he had, he was rearranging the things he had brought from home in his tuck-box, and once, not long after he became my fag, I found him at the end of a corridor one dreary Saturday afternoon, with the autumn rain pouring down outside, trying to set fire to a pile of newspapers stacked on the stone floor beside the open door which led into a back yard. I saw his small, crouched figure in the grey light behind him, and the little flames licking around the edges of the newspaper, but the fire would not burn properly. When I asked what he thought he was doing, he said he wanted to make a huge blaze, and would not mind if the whole school were reduced to a pile of rubble and ashes. After that I kept an eye on Gerald. I let him off tidying my room and cleaning my boots, and I made the tea myself and shared it with him, a breach of regulations regarded with disapproval by most of my fellow pupils and my house-master himself, rather as if it were against the natural order of things. In the evenings Gerald often accompanied me to the dark-room where, at this time, I was making my first experiments with photography. This little cubby-hole behind the chemistry lab had not been used for years, but the wall cupboards and drawers still held several boxes with rolls of film, a large supply of photographic paper and a miscellaneous collection of cameras, including an Ensign such as I myself owned later. From the outset my main concern was with the shape and the self-contained nature of discrete things, the curve of banisters on a staircase, the moulding of a stone arch over a gateway, the tangled precision of the blades in a tussock of dried grass. I took hundreds of such photographs at Stower Grange, most of them in square format, but it never seemed to me

right to turn the viewfinder of my camera on people. In my photographic work I was always especially entranced, said Austerlitz, by the moment when the shadows of reality, so to speak, emerge out of nothing on the exposed paper, as memories do in the middle of the night, darkening again if you try to cling to them, just like a photographic print left in the developing bath too long. Gerald enjoyed helping me, and I can still see him, a head shorter than I was, standing beside me in the dark-room, which was dimly illuminated only by the little reddish light, holding the photographs in tweezers and swishing them back and forth in a sink full of water. He often told me about his family on these occasions, and most of all he liked talking about the three homing pigeons who would be expecting his return, he thought, as eagerly as he usually awaited theirs. Gerald's Uncle Alphonso had given him these pigeons a year ago for his tenth birthday, said Austerlitz, two of them a slaty blue, one snow-white. Whenever possible, if someone was going to Bala or Aberystwyth by car, he would send his three pigeons to be freed at a distance, and they always infallibly found their way back to their loft. Once, towards the end of last summer, Tilly the white pigeon did stay away much longer than the homeward flight should have taken her, after being dispatched on a test flight from Dolgellau only a few miles up the valley, and it was not until the following day, when he was on the point of giving up hope, that she finally returned – on foot, walking up the gravel drive with a broken wing. I often thought later of this tale of the bird making her long journey home alone, wondering how she had managed to reach her destination over the steep terrain, circumventing numerous obstacles, and that question, said Austerlitz, a question which still exercises my mind today when I see a pigeon

W. G. Sebald

in flight, is one that, against all reason, seems to me connected with the way Gerald finally lost his life. – I believe, Austerlitz went on after some considerable time, it was on the second or third parents' visiting day that Gerald, proud of his privileged relationship with me, introduced me to his mother Adela. She can hardly have been thirty at the time, and she was very glad that after his initial difficulties her young son had found a protector in me. Gerald had already told me about his father Aldous, shot down over the Ardennes in the last winter of the war, and I had also heard how his mother was now living with only an old uncle and an even older great-uncle in a country house just outside the small seaside town of Barmouth. Gerald claimed that its position was the finest anywhere along the entire Welsh coast. Once Adela had discovered from Gerald that I had no parents or any family at all, I was invited to their house repeatedly, indeed constantly, even when I was doing my national service and when I was up at Oxford, and I could wish now, said Austerlitz, to have vanished without trace in the peace that always reigned there. At the very beginning of the school holidays, when we travelled westward up the Dee valley in the little steam train from Wrexham, I would feel my heart begin to lift. Bend after bend, our train followed the winding of the river, the green meadows looked in through the open carriage window, and so did the houses, stony grey or whitewashed, the gleaming slate roofs, the silver shades of the willows, the darker alder woods, the sheep-pastures climbing up beyond the trees, and higher still the mountains, sometimes tinged with blue, and the sky where the clouds, coming in from the sea, always drove eastwards. Scraps of steam vapour flew past outside; you could hear the engine whistling and feel the air cool on your forehead. Never have I travelled better, said Austerlitz, than on this journey of seventy miles at the most, which took us three and a half hours. When we stopped at Bala, the half way station, of course I could not help thinking back to my time in the manse, visible up there on its hill, yet it always seemed to me inconceivable that I had really been among its unhappy inhabitants for almost the whole of my life. And every time I set eyes on Lake Bala, particularly when its surface was churned up by the wind in winter, I remembered the story Evan the cobbler had told me, about the two headstreams of Dwy Fawr and Dwy Fach which are said to flow right through the lake, far down in its dark depths, never mingling their waters with its own. The two rivers, according to Evan, said Austerlitz, were called after the only human beings not drowned but saved from the biblical deluge in the distant past. At the far end of Lake Bala the railway line passed over a low anticline into the Afon Mawddach valley. The mountains were higher now, coming down closer and closer to the tracks until you reached Dolgellau, where they retreated again, and gentler slopes fell to the estuary of the Mawddach, which reaches far inland like a fjord. Finally, when we left the southern bank and crawled to the opposite side over the bridge, almost a mile long and supported on mighty posts of oak, on our right the river bed, inundated by the sea at high tide and looking like a mountain lake, and on our left

Barmouth Bay stretching to the bright horizon, I felt so joyful that I often scarcely knew where to look first. Adela used to fetch us from Barmouth station, usually in the little black-painted pony-trap, and then it was only half an hour before the gravel of the drive up to Andromeda Lodge was crunching under our wheels, the bay pony stopped, and we could get down and enter into our holiday refuge. The two-storey house, built of pale-grey brick, was protected to the north and north-east by the Llawr Llech hills, which fall steeply away at this point. To the south-west the terrain lay open in a wide semi-circle, so that from the forecourt of the house you had a view of the full length of the estuary from Dolgellau to Barmouth, while these places themselves were excluded from the panorama, which was almost devoid of human habitations, by a rocky outcrop on one side and a laurel-grown hill on the other. Only on the far side of the river could the little village of Arthog be seen – in certain atmospheric conditions, said Austerlitz, you might have thought it an eternity away – infinitesimally small, with the shadowy side of Cader Idris rising behind it to a height of almost three thousand feet above the shimmering sea. While the climate of the entire area was remarkably mild, temperatures in this especially favoured place were a couple of degrees higher even than the Barmouth average. The garden, which had run completely wild during the war years and went up the slope at the back of the house, contained plants and shrubs that I had never seen in Wales before: giant rhubarb and New Zealand ferns taller than a grown man, water lettuce and camellias, thickets of bamboo and palms. And a brook tumbled down over a rocky wall to the valley, its white spray constantly pervading the dappled twilight under the leafy canopy of the tall trees. But it was not only the plants, natives of warmer climates, that made you feel you were living in another world: the greatest exotic attractions of Andromeda Lodge were the white cockatoos which flew all around the house within a radius of up to two or three miles, calling from the bushes, bathing and luxuriating in the fine spray from the cascading brook until evening fell. Gerald's great-grandfather had brought several pairs home from the Moluccas and established them in the orangery, where they soon increased and multiplied, forming a large colony. They lived in small sherry casks that had been stacked on top of each other in a pyramid against one of the side walls, and departing from their native custom, said Austerlitz, they had lined these casks themselves with wood-shavings from a sawmill down beside the river. Most of them even survived the hard winter of 1947, since Adela kept the old orangery stove heated for them through the two icy months of January and February. It was wonderful, said Austerlitz, to see the dexterity with which the birds clambered around the trelliswork, hanging on by their beaks, and performing all kinds of acrobatic feats as they came down; to watch them flying in and out of the open windows or hopping and walking along the ground, always active and always, or that was the impression they gave, intent upon some purpose or other. In fact they were very like human beings in many ways. You might hear them sigh, laugh, sneeze and yawn. They cleared their throats before beginning to converse in their own cockatoo language, they showed themselves alert, scheming, mischievous and sly, deceitful, malicious, vindictive and quarrelsome. They liked certain people, particularly Adela and Gerald, and persecuted others with downright malice, for instance the Welsh housekeeper who seldom showed her face out of doors. They seemed to know exactly when she would be going to chapel, always wearing a black hat and carrying a black umbrella, and on these occasions they lay in wait to screech at her in the most obnoxious way. They also reflected human society in the way they ganged up together in ever-changing groups, or then again paired off in couples sitting side by side as if they knew nothing but harmony and were forever inseparable. They even had their own cemetery, with a long row of graves in a clearing surrounded by strawberry trees, and one of the rooms on the upper floor of Andromeda Lodge had in it what was obviously a purpose-built wall cupboard, full of dark-green cardboard boxes containing a number of dead birds of species related to the cockatoos, their red-chested or yellow-headed brothers, Hyacinth and Scarlet Macaws, Ruby Lorikeets and Blue-winged Parrotlets, Horned Parakeets and Ground Parrots, all brought back by Gerald's great-grandfather or great-great-grandfather from his circumnavigation of the globe, or alternatively ordered from a trader called Théodore Grace in Le Havre for a few guineas or louis d'or, as noted on the provenances placed inside the boxes. The finest of all these birds, in a collection which also included some native woodpeckers, wrynecks, kites and orioles, was the African Grey Parrot. I can still see the inscription on his green cardboard sarcophagus: Jaco, *Ps. erithacus L*. He came from the Congo and had reached the great age of sixty-six in his Welsh exile, as his obituary recounted, adding that he had been very tame and trusting, was a quick learner, chattered away to himself and others, could whistle entire songs and had composed some too, but best of all he liked to mimic the voices of children and to have them teach him new words. His one bad habit was that if no one gave him any apricot kernels and hard nuts, which he could crack open with the greatest ease, he went about in a bad temper chewing and shredding the furniture. Gerald often took this special parrot out of his box. He was about nine inches long, and as his name suggests had ash-grey plumage, as well as a carmine tail, a black beak, and a pale face that you might have thought was marked by deep grief. Indeed, Austerlitz went on, there was some kind of cabinet of natural curiosities in almost every room at Andromeda Lodge: cases with multiple drawers, some of them glass-fronted, where the roundish eggs of parrots were arranged in their hundreds; collections of shells, minerals, beetles and butterflies; slowworms, adders and lizards preserved in formaldehyde; snail shells and sea urchins, crabs and shrimps, and large herbaria containing leaves, flowers and grasses. Adela had once told him, said Austerlitz, that the transformation of Andromeda Lodge into a kind of natural-history museum had begun in 1869, when Gerald's parrot-collecting ancestor made the acquaintance of Charles Darwin, then working on his

study of the Descent of Man in a rented house not far from Dolgellau. Darwin had paid frequent visits to the Fitzpatricks of Andromeda Lodge in those days, and according to a family tradition he always praised the wonderful view from the house. It was from the same period, according to Adela, said Austerlitz, that the schism in the Fitzpatrick clan dated, a schism continuing to the present day, whereby one of the two sons in every generation abandoned the Catholic faith and became a natural scientist. For instance Aldous, Gerald's father, had been a botanist, while his brother Evelyn, over twenty years his senior, clung to the traditional Papist creed regarded in Wales as the worst of all perversions. In fact the Catholic line of the family had always been represented by its crazier and more eccentric members, as the case of Uncle Evelyn clearly illustrated. At the time when I was spending many weeks every year with the Fitzpatricks as Gerald's guest, said

Austerlitz, Evelyn was perhaps in his mid-fifties, but was so crippled by Bechterew's disease that he looked like an old man, and could walk only with the greatest difficulty, bending right over. For that very reason, however, and to prevent his joints from seizing up entirely, he was always on the move in his rooms on the top floor, where a kind of handrail had been fitted along the walls, like the barre in a ballet school. He held on to this handrail as he inched his way forward, moaning quietly, his head and bent torso scarcely higher than his hand on the rail. It took him a good hour to make the rounds of his quarters, from the bedroom into the living-room, out of the living-room into the corridor, and from the corridor back to the bedroom. Gerald, who had already developed an aversion to the Roman faith, once claimed, said Austerlitz, that Uncle Evelyn had grown so crooked out of sheer miserliness, which he justified to himself by reflecting that he sent the money he did not spend in any given week, usually amounting to twelve or thirteen shillings, as a donation to the Mission to the Congo for the salvation of black souls still languishing in unbelief. There were no curtains or other furnishings in Evelyn's rooms, since he did not want to make unnecessary use of anything, even if it had been acquired long ago and simply had to be brought from another part of the house. Years before, he had had a narrow strip of linoleum laid on the wooden floor where he walked beside the walls, to spare the wood, and his dragging footsteps had worn the linoleum so thin that you could make out almost nothing of its original flower pattern. Not until the

temperature on the thermometer beside the window had dropped to below fifty degrees Fahrenheit for several days running was the housekeeper allowed to light a tiny fire in the hearth, a fire burning almost no fuel at all. To save electricity, Evelyn always went to bed when darkness fell, which meant around four in the afternoon in winter, although lying down was perhaps even more painful for him than walking, so that as a rule, despite his exhausted state after his constant perambulations, it was a long time before he could get to sleep. Then, through the grille of a ventilation shaft that linked his bedchamber to one of the ground-floor living-rooms and inadvertently functioned as a kind of communication channel, he could be heard calling on numerous different saints for hours on end, in particular, if I remember correctly, Saints Catherine and Elizabeth, who suffered the most cruel of martyrdoms, begging them to intercede for him in the contingency, as he put it, of his imminent appearance before the judgment seat of his Heavenly Lord. Unlike Uncle Evelyn, said Austerlitz after a while, taking from his jacket pocket a kind of folder containing several post-card-sized photographs, Great-Uncle Alphonso, who was about ten years older and continued the line of the naturalist Fitzpatricks, looked positively youthful. Always even-tempered, he spent most of his time out of doors, going on long expeditions even in the worst of weather, or when it was fine sitting on a camp stool somewhere near the house in his white smock, a straw hat on his head, painting watercolours. When he was thus engaged he generally wore glasses with grey silk

tissue instead of lenses in the frames, so that the landscape appeared through a fine veil that muted its
colours, and the weight of the world dissolved before
your eyes. The faint images that Alphonso transferred
on to paper, said Austerlitz, were barely sketches of
pictures – here a rocky slope, there a small bosky thicket
or a cumulus cloud – fragments, almost without colour,
fixed with a tint made of a few drops of water and a
grain of malachite green or ash blue. I remember, said
Austerlitz, how Alphonso once told his great-nephew
and me that everything was fading before our eyes, and
that many of the loveliest of colours had already disappeared, or existed only where no one saw them, in the
submarine gardens fathoms deep below the surface of
the sea. In his childhood, he said, he used to walk beside
the chalk cliffs of Devon and Cornwall, where hollows
and basins have been carved and cut out of the rock by
the breakers over millions of years, admiring the endless
diversity of the semi-sentient marvels oscillating
between the vegetable, animal and mineral kingdoms,
the zooids and corallines, sea anemones, sea fans and
sea feathers, the anthozoans and crustaceans over which
the tide washed twice a day while long fronds of
seaweed swayed around them, and which then, as the
water went out, revealed their wonderfully iridescent
life in the rock pools exposed once more to the light
and the air, showing all the colours of the rainbow –
emerald, scarlet and rosy red, sulphur yellow, velvety
black. At that time the whole south-west coast of the
island was surrounded by a colourful fringe ebbing and
flowing with the tides, and now, said Uncle Alphonso,

barely half a century later, those glories had been almost entirely destroyed by our passion for collecting and by other imponderable disturbances and disruptions. On another occasion, said Austerlitz, Great-Uncle Alphonso took us up the hill behind the house on a still, moonless night to spend a few hours looking into the mysterious world of moths. Most of us, said Austerlitz, know nothing about moths except that they eat holes in carpets and clothes and have to be kept at bay by the use of camphor and naphthalene, although in truth their lineage is among the most ancient and most remarkable in the whole history of nature. Soon after darkness fell we were sitting on a promontory far above Andromeda Lodge, behind us the higher slopes and before us the immense darkness out at sea, and no sooner had Alphonso placed his incandescent lamp in a shallow hollow surrounded by heather and lit it than the moths, not one of which we had seen during our climb, came flying in as if from nowhere, describing thousands of different arcs and spirals and loops, until like snowflakes they formed a silent storm around the light, while others, wings whirring, crawled over the sheet spread under the lamp or else, exhausted by their wild circling, settled in the grey recesses of the egg boxes stacked in a crate by Alphonso to provide shelter for them. I do remember, said Austerlitz, that the two of us, Gerald and I, could not get over our amazement at the endless variety of these invertebrates, which are usually hidden from our sight, and that Alphonso let us simply gaze at their wonderful display for a long time, but I don't recollect now exactly what kinds of night-winged creatures landed there beside us, perhaps they were China-Marks, Dark Porcelains and Marbled Beauties, Scarce Silverlines or Burnished Brass, Green Foresters and Green Adelas, White Plumes, Light Arches, Old Ladies and Ghost Moths, but at any rate we counted dozens of them, so different in structure and appearance that neither Gerald nor I could grasp it all. Some had collars and cloaks, like elegant gentlemen on their way to the opera, said Gerald; some had a plain basic hue, but when they moved their wings showed a fantastic lining underneath, with oblique and wavy lines, shadows, crescent markings and lighter patches, freckles, zigzag bands, fringes and veining and colours you could never have imagined, moss green shot with blue, fox brown, saffron, lime yellow, satiny white, and a metallic gleam as of powdered brass or gold. Many of them were still resplendent in immaculate garments, others, their short lives almost over, had torn and ragged wings. Alphonso told us how each of these extravagant creatures had its own character, and that many of them lived only among alders, or on hot, stony slopes, in pastures on poor soil, or on moors. Describing their previous existence as larvae, he said that almost all cater-pillars ate only one kind of food – the roots of couch grass, the leaves of sallow or barberry, withered bram-ble foliage – and they stuffed themselves with that chosen food, said Alphonso, until they became well-nigh senseless, whereas the moths ate nothing more at all for the rest of their lives, and were bent solely on the busi-ness of reproduction. They did sometimes seem to suffer thirst, and in periods of drought, when no dew had fallen at night for a long time, it was apparently known for them to set out together in a kind of cloud in search of the nearest river or stream, where they drowned in large numbers as they tried to settle on the flowing water. And I also remember what Alphonso said about the extraordinarily keen hearing of moths, said Austerlitz. They can make out the squeaking of bats from a great distance, and he, Alphonso, had himself noticed that in the evening, when the housekeeper came out into the yard to call her cat Enid in that shrill voice of hers, they always rose from the bushes and flew away into the darker trees. During the day, said Alphonso, they slept safely hidden under stones, or in cracks in the rock, in leaf litter on the ground or among foliage. Most of them are in a death-like state when you find them, and have to coax and quiver themselves back to life, crawling over the ground and jerkily moving their wings and legs before they are ready for flight. Their body temperature will then be thirty-six degrees, like that of mammals, and of dolphins and tunny fish swimming at full speed. Thirty-six degrees, according to Alphonso, has always proved the best natural level, a kind of magical threshold, and it had sometimes occurred to him, Alphonso, said Austerlitz, that all mankind's misfortunes were connected with its departure at some point in time from that norm, and with the slightly feverish, overheated condition in which we constantly found ourselves. On that summer night, said Austerlitz, we sat high above the estuary of the Mawddach in our hollow in the hills until daybreak, watching the moths fly to us, perhaps some ten thousand of them by Alphonso's estimate. The trails of light which they seemed to leave behind them in all kinds of curlicues and streamers and spirals, and which Gerald in particular admired, did not really exist, explained Alphonso, but were merely phantom traces created by the sluggish reaction of the human eye, appearing to see a certain afterglow in the place from which the insect itself, shining for only the fraction of a second in the lamplight, had already gone. It was such unreal phenomena, said Alphonso, the sudden incursion of unreality into the real world, certain effects of light in the landscape spread out before us, or in the eye of a beloved person, that kindled our deepest feelings, or at least what we took for them. Although I did not study natural history later, said Austerlitz, many of Great-Uncle Alphonso's botanical and zoological disquisitions have remained in my mind. Only a few days ago I was re-reading that passage in Darwin he once showed me, describing a flock of butterflies flying uninterruptedly for several hours ten miles out from the South American coast, when even with a telescope it was impossible to find a patch of empty sky visible between their whirling wings. But I always found what Alphonso told us at that time about the life and death of moths especially memorable, and of all creatures I still feel the greatest awe for them. In the warmer months of the year one or other of those nocturnal insects quite often strays indoors from the small garden behind my house. When I get up early in the morning, I find them clinging to the wall, motionless. I believe, said Austerlitz, they know they have lost their way, since if you do not put them out again carefully they will stay where they are, never moving, until the last breath is out of their bodies, and indeed they will remain in the place where they came to grief even after death, held fast by the tiny claws that stiffened in their last agony,

until a draught of air detaches them and blows them into a dusty corner. Sometimes, seeing one of these moths that have met their end in my house, I wonder what kind of fear and pain they feel while they are lost. As Alphonso had told him, said Austerlitz, there is really no reason to suppose that lesser beings are devoid of sentient life. We are not alone in dreaming at night for, quite apart from dogs and other domestic creatures whose emotions have been bound up with ours for many thousands of years, the smaller mammals such as mice and moles also live in a world that exists only in their minds whilst they are asleep, as we can detect from their eye movements, and who knows, said Austerlitz, perhaps moths dream as well, perhaps a lettuce in the garden dreams as it looks up at the moon by night. I myself often felt as if I were dreaming during those weeks and months I spent at the Fitzpatricks' house, said Austerlitz, even in daylight. The view from the room with the blue ceiling which Adela always called mine did indeed verge on the unreal. I looked down from above on the treetops, mainly of cedars and parasol pines and resembling a green, hilly landscape going down from the road below the house to the river bank, I saw the dark folds of the mountain range on the other side of the river, and I spent hours looking out at the Irish Sea that was always changing with the time of day and the weather. How often I stood by the open window, unable to think coherently in the face of this spectacle, which was never the same twice. In the morning you saw the shadowy half of the world outside, the grey of the air lying in layers above the water. In the afternoon cumulus clouds often rose on the south-west horizon, their snow-white slopes and steep precipices displacing one another, towering above each other, reaching higher and higher, as high, Gerald once commented, said Austerlitz, as the peaks of the Andes or the Karakorum Mountains. Or you might see rain falling in the distance, drawn inland from the sea like heavy curtains drawn in a theatre, and on autumn evenings mist would roll on to the beach, accumulating by the mountain sides and forcing its way up the valley. But on bright summer days, in particular, so evenly disposed a lustre lay over the whole of Barmouth Bay that the separate surfaces of sand and water, sea and land, earth and sky could no longer be distinguished. All forms and colours were dissolved in a pearl-grey haze; there were no contrasts, no shading any more, only flowing transitions with the light throbbing through them, a single blur from which only the most fleeting of visions emerged, and strangely – I remember this well – it was the very evanescence of those visions that gave me, at the time, something like a sense of eternity. One evening, after we had done some shopping in Barmouth, Adela, Gerald, the dog Toby and I went out on the long footbridge running beside the railway line which, as I mentioned before, said Austerlitz, crosses the estuary of the Mawddach at this point, where it is over a mile wide. For a halfpenny each you could sit there on one of the seats protected on three sides, like little cabins, from wind and weather, with your back to the land and looking out to sea. It was the end of a fine day in late summer, the fresh salty air blew around us, and in the evening light the tide came in, gleaming like a dense shoal of mackerel, flowing under the bridge and up the river, so swift and strong that you might have thought you were going the other way, out to the open sea in a boat. We all four sat there together in silence until the sun had set. Even the usually restless Toby, who had the same odd ruff of hair around his face as the little dog belonging to the girl in the Vyrnwy photograph, did not move at our feet, but looked up, rapt, at the heights where the light still lingered and large numbers of swallows were swooping through the air. After a while, when the dark dots had become tinier and tinier in their arching flight, Gerald asked whether we knew that these voyagers never slept on the earth. Once they had left their nests, he said, picking up Toby and tickling him under the chin, they never touched the ground again. As night fell they would rise two or three miles in the air and glide there, banking now to one side, now to the other, and moving their outspread wings only occasionally, until they came back down to us at break of day.

POCKET PENGUINS

POCKET PENGUINS